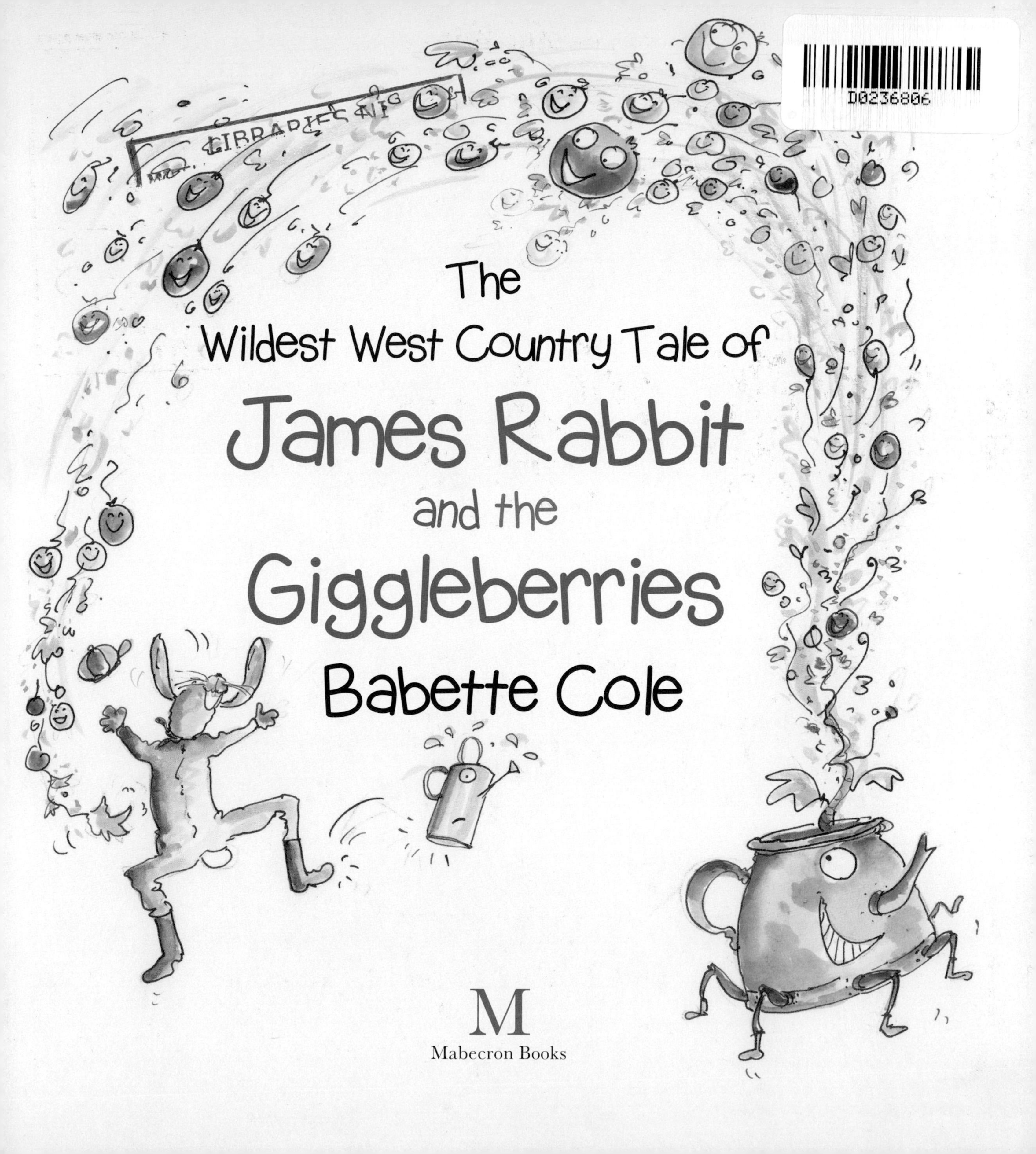

The Wildest West Country Tale of James Rabbit and the Giggleberries

Babette Cole

M
Mabecron Books

Once upon a hill in the West Country, there lived a tall skinny bunny

called James Rabbit.

Because James had such long ears he could not get a job anywhere except for those mean old weasels, The Measly Brothers, who farmed the red hills thereabouts. They only paid him one penny a week for driving tractors full of cow poo,

from dawn until dusk!

This was *not* enough to feed his hungry baby bunnies, let alone buy them tiny
said his wife Pearl.

worsted waistcoats to keep them warm. "You'll have to get a bank loan,"

So he went to see
slimy Mr Walter Croaker, who owned the River Bank, to see if he could borrow some money.

That nasty old toad refused to give him a loan and told him to sell his fluffy baby bunnies to be made into fur coats and matching handbags
instead!

When James Rabbit told Pearl
she was very
ANGRY,
WHAT!
she said,
"That mean old toad will
get his comeuppance,
you mark my words."

Lord and Lady Brockenhurst were advertising for a part-time cook, so she put on her best bonnet, left her baby bunnies with her cousin Ruby, and made her way up to Sett House.

Lord and Lady Brockenhurst were filthy rich because they owned a string of fun parks by the seaside. They were very smelly, had disgusting table manners, and grinned a lot.

Pearl got the job. She found it hard to cook for Badgers, being a vegetarian herself, but they loved her worm flavoured chocolate ice cream.

One morning, when she was hanging out the tea towels in the walled garden at the back of the great house,

she noticed a broken down old greenhouse.

This gave her an idea.

“If it pleases your Lord and Ladyship,” she says politely, wiping her paws on her pinny like a good bunny should, “but could my husband James grow some carrots in that old greenhouse, for our baby bunnies?”

“Yuss, yuss,” grunted the Brockenhursts.

“As long as there’s plenty of worms in the compost for our ice cream.”

Pearl rushed back to the burrow to tell her husband the good news.

James was delighted, "I'll start tonight!" he said.

He was too poor to
afford extra
candles

so the glow worms said they would help.
There was no money for pots to
grow seeds in either.
"Will we do, James Rabbit?"
said some rusty old
kettles and buckets.
Even Jennifer Hopper
gave him some sticky
frog spawn to mend
the broken glass.

He wheeled the lot up to the greenhouse.

On the way Mr Oakley Ash gave him some leaf mould.

Now all he needed was some cow poo for making the compost, and of course some carrot seed.

Soon the greenhouse
was as good as new.

The next day at work James asked his boss if he could have some cow poo.

The mean old weasel said, "yes" but he would deduct it from his wages.

So the cows gave him some for free!

James worked
hard in the
greenhouse
every night.
He made lovely
compost with
loads of juicy
worms for
Pearl's ice cream.

The
Brockenhursts
were so
pleased they
gave him
a silver sixpence
to buy
carrot
seed.

So, on Saturday he caught the bus to Carroton Farmers Market. James Rabbit did not know what carrot seed looked like but he went ahead and bought some 'carrot seed' from those twisted squirrel sisters, Salome and Delilah Acorn.

(who should have known better)

James planted the seeds that very night
by glow worm light.
When the stars shone brightly he sang a song
he had made up all on his own.
The owls, nightjars, crickets
and rats and mice
all joined in.

"Little seeds, little seeds, grow and grow and grow. Make lovely juicy carrots
tummies. For I'm a father rabbit, doing the best I know."

that I can weed and hoe. Please feed my baby bunnies, and fill their hungry

BUT LATER,

when he came back to water
them whatever he had planted
were definitely not carrots!
They looked like berries,

and
they were making a
"rustling sort of giggling noise.

When James took a closer look they reached out with their vine-like arms and tickled him until he went into fits of uncontrollable giggles!

As carrots they were a disaster but he was laughing, dancing and singing so much he forgot about that!

"What be
them
things?"
scolded
Pearl.
"I cannot
feed my
babies
on that!"

But they tickled her into
such a giggle she told James
they should take them to
Carroton,

to cheer up all those sad
little creatures Slimy Croaker
had diddled out of their money.

And that's exactly what they did, right outside the River Bank!

Meanwhile Pearl had another idea for the Giggleberries.

Carroton went crazy. Everyone, including James's bosses loved the Giggleberries. The tickling caused such merriment they forgot about the bank manager and just had fun.

James's older children had a busking bunny band, they played such good Bunny Hop the whole market place was rocking!

It turned into the wildest street party the West Country had ever seen.

Hippy Hoppin
Let's Go to the Hop
Hop
Hop Hop
Ho Ho Ho
Ha Ha Ha
giggle giggle

Slimy Walter Croaker was hopping mad!
He hated seeing anyone have fun,
"I'll give you a loan, James Rabbit,"
he yelled, "If you stop giving those
things away outside my bank!"

But he slipped on a bunch of Giggleberries and tumbled head first into a pram full of them which Pearl happened to be wheeling past at the time. They tickled him so hard he blew awful smelly, toady

Bubble Bum
Bubbles.

"Thank you, your honour, Sir," giggled James Rabbit. "But I does not need a loan no more, for if I can make folk as happy as this with my Giggleberries, well then I'm as rich as a

BiLLionhare!"

Indeed the Giggleberries had tickled Slimy Croaker into a much nicer happier toad.

"I know!" he laughed, "Let's make everyone Happy Happy Happy. I'll give all the Bank's money away!"

Ha Ha Hee Hee Ha Ha Ho Ho Ho

He did not know that Pearl had asked the Brockenhursts to employ James to grow his berries for their fun fair.

Although their Bubble Bum clouds hid the sun sometimes, the tourists flocked to Bunny Salterton because they were crazy about The Giggleberries!

And

as for the baby bunnies

Well, they never went hungry

again!

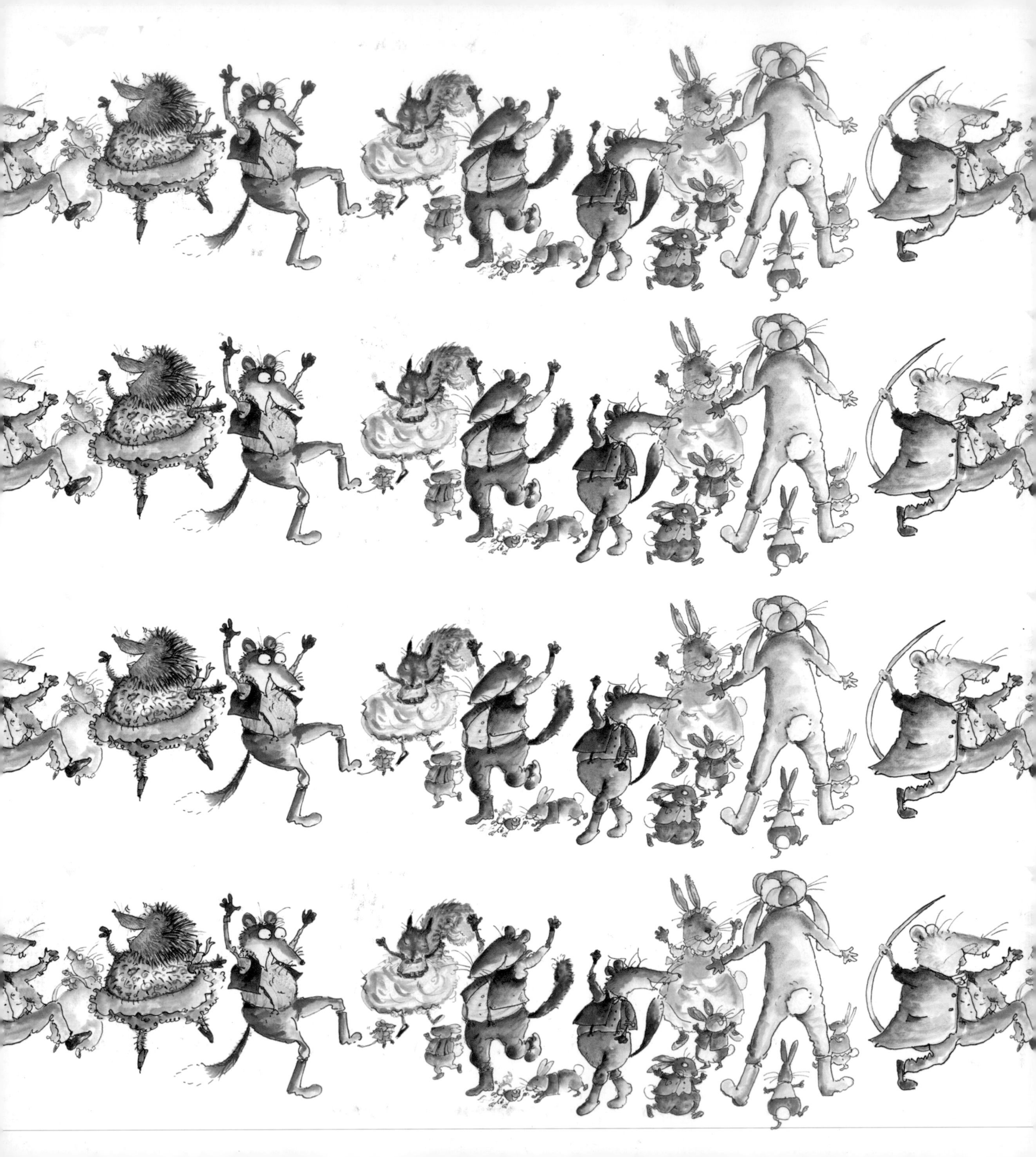